THE FIFTH GRADE READER

A Fun 5th Grade Chapter Book with 12 Short Stories for Kids Ages 10-12

CURIOUS BEE

ISBN: 979-8-89095-042-0

Table of Contents

ATTENTION:

DO YOU WANT MY FUTURE BOOKS AT HEAVY DISCOUNTS AND EVEN FOR FREE?

HEAD OVER TO <u>WWW.SECRETREADS.COM</u> AND JOIN MY SECRET BOOK CLUB!

Introduction

Stories are an excellent source of information and spark our imagination. Fiction and non-fiction tales take us to far-off places we've only dreamed about. A good story teaches us about the world around us because stories take us to other countries, far beyond the past, down deep in the ocean, and to outer space. There is no limit to what stories can teach us when we read!

As a story expands our understanding of the world, it broadens our vocabulary and builds our understanding of people, places, events, and things. A story may encourage us to learn something new.

The stories in this book are specially crafted for readers at the fifth-grade level; ages nine through eleven. Readers will be met with the appropriate number of challenges in learning new words, building reading comprehension skills, and deciphering more complex sentence structures. They are designed for independent reading, but some readers may enjoy adults reading to them!

Studies show that children who are regularly read to, have a better grasp of language including vocabulary, syntax, grammar, and comprehension. Secondly, children who hear stories frequently have more developed social-emotional skills, are better problem solvers and perform better at school. So don't be shy about asking an adult to read to you!

Because everyone develops differently, some of these stories may be simple to read while others may have some challenging words. Overall, however, most fifth graders reading on-level should be able to read our tales. When you come across an unfamiliar word, use context clues to decipher its meaning. Dictionaries are a great tool to have! Or you can download a dictionary app to your phone or tablet.

If you are in, soon to be in, or just finished fifth grade, this book is for you! Do your best to decode and read new words you come across using the context and pictures to understand their meaning.

As a bonus, we've included a list of open-ended questions you can ask yourself before, during, or after reading a story. These questions will promote critical thinking, enhance comprehension, and further develop language and literacy skills. Each story also has three to five comprehension questions specific to that tale included at the end.

We hope you enjoy reading these engaging fifth-grade stories as much as we enjoyed creating them for you!

Happy reading!

Open-Ended Questions to Ask Before, During, or After Reading

Each of the following questions is designed to promote critical thinking, problem-solving, social-emotional skills, and language and literacy skills.

For adults reading with kids, feel free to adapt the language of the questions as needed to your child's age and developmental level and based on the story!

Questions to Ask Before Reading

1. Looking at the picture, what do you think this story is about? Why? What clues does the picture give you?
2. Based on the title, what do you think this story is about?
3. If you've read this story before, do you remember what happens in this story?

Questions to Ask During Reading

1. What do you think will happen next? Why? What clues do you have?
2. Do you agree with the character's choices? Why or why not?
3. How do you think the story will end? Why?
4. What could (the character) do differently?
5. What would you do if you were in this situation?

Questions to Ask After

1. Before we started you said you thought the story was about (blank). Were you correct? Why or why not?
2. Did you enjoy this story? Why or why not?
3. What was your favorite part of the story? Why?
4. What was your least favorite part of the story? Why?
5. Can you think of another story you know that is like this one? What do they have in common? What is the difference between the two?
6. Who was your favorite character? Why?
7. Do you think the characters solved the problem well? Why or why not?
8. How would you have solved the problem in this story?
9. Was the story fiction or non-fiction? How do you know?

    a. Fiction means made up or not real.
    b. Non-fiction means a true story.

The Astronomer's Tower

Chapter One

In a far-away town, on a far-away island, in the middle of an ocean you've probably never heard of, there sits a tall stone tower. The tower is made from a mismatch of stones and rocks, some gray, some brown, some white, and some black. It is a circular tower reaching up towards the sky.

Despite what many people visiting the island for the first time think, this tower is not a lighthouse. Although it is easy to understand why it would be mistaken as one. The tower is so tall, it is often the first thing people notice when approaching the island by boat.

However, unlike a lighthouse, which has a top encircled in glass with a bright, shining, light inside, this tower is dark at the top. There are eight large windows around the top, but there is no glass inside them. Instead, peeking out of each window is a telescope aimed at different parts of the sky.

You see, this tower is an astronomy tower. And it doesn't belong to just any astronomer, it belongs to the greatest astronomer in any kingdom near or far. The small island, in the middle of the far-away ocean, is called Trindleview. Trindleview is ruled by a kind king and a generous queen who are both amateur scientists.

The king and queen love science so much that they hold an annual science fair, and they employ scientists of every kind and discipline to work for them and make the latest discoveries.

But of all the sciences the king and queen love, they adore astronomy the most. The royal couple dreams of visiting the stars and distant planets and galaxies and often stares with wonder at the nighttime sky.

The king and queen love the nighttime sky so much, that when they married, they held their wedding ceremony at midnight under the stars and a full moon!

For many years, ever since the queen was a young girl and her mother and father ruled the kingdom, the royal astronomer was Sir Rufus Hubbard.

Sir Hubbard was a brilliant astronomer who discovered two new planets and five new stars during his years. Before him, his father was the royal astronomer and before his father, his grandmother.

Sir Hubbard's family had been the royal astronomers as far back any anyone could remember. Every history book in Trindleview mentioned Sir Hubbard's family.

But now there was a problem. Sir Hubbard was very old and ready to retire. And unlike his family before him, Sir Hubbard never married and did not have any children. The king and queen pondered how could they find a new royal astronomer.

Chapter Two

The king and queen wanted to honor Sir Hubbard's request to retire, but they asked him if they could have three months to find a replacement. He generously granted their wish.

The king and queen sat in their throne room and discussed the problem; they were scientific thinkers, so they knew there had to be a sensible solution!

"What if, we simply ask around the kingdom to see if anyone would like to be the astronomer?" Asked the king.

"We could," said the queen, "but how will we know whether or not they are a good astronomer?"

"True, true," said the king. "Maybe we could write to our neighboring kingdoms and ask if they have a spare astronomer?"

"We could," said the queen, "but what if our neighbors think we are trying to steal their best astronomer and start a war?"

"Ah, that would be a problem," said the king. "Then perhaps we should hold our annual science fair with an astronomy theme and choose the winner from there!"

The queen clapped her hands and exclaimed, "That is an excellent idea! That way, contestants won't know they are interviewing for a job. It will let us see the very best astronomers from all over the world."

So, with that, it was decided. The king and queen announced the science fair to be held in three months would be astronomy-based.

The announcement proclaimed they wanted to see the most innovative and interesting science projects - projects that were new and had never been seen before!

The announcement was sent to every corner of Earth in the hope that a young and talented astronomer would enter the contest and take on the role of Trindleview's royal astronomer.

Chapter Three

As the days inched closer to the science fair, the queen spent more and more time atop the astronomer's tower with Sir Hubbard. She had known him her whole life. He was like a grandfather to her, and she was going to miss him very much when he retired.

The queen often went to the tower even when Sir Hubbard wasn't there. She found peace and quiet at the top of the tower, and it allowed her to think more clearly when she faced a problem.

On the night before the science fair, the queen couldn't sleep so she climbed the tower's many stairs and looked out at the stars. She sighed, deep in her thoughts. The queen was feeling anxious. What if no one was talented enough to replace Sir Hubbard? What if they had already discovered everything there was to know about space? However, the queen easily dismissed that thought as impossible. She *knew* there was so much more to learn. She had another thought: What if she didn't like the most talented astronomer? Just because someone was smart and talented didn't mean she would like them.

All these thoughts and more swirled in the queen's brain, then she heard footsteps behind her.

"What troubles you, my dear?" Said Sir Hubbard.

The queen sighed again and said, "I know you must retire. You have served as a wonderful royal astronomer. But you are like family, and I have come to think of this tower as your home. It will feel strange to have someone new working here."

"It will be different, yes," Sir Hubbard replied. "But different isn't always bad. Each day the sun sets and the moon rises, and it is always a little different than the day before. We see this in the pattern of the moon. A new astronomer is simply a new moon rising. It will shine and look a little different but works much in the same way."

The queen nodded her head and hugged Sir Hubbard, then she set off to bed. Tomorrow was going to be a very big day, and she needed to get at least a few hours of sleep.

Chapter Four

The sun rose at exactly 7:32 the next morning, but the palace and the surrounding grounds were already full of life. Many of the science fair entrants had arrived the day before and spent the night as guests of the king and queen. Only those coming from a few miles away were arriving today.

All around the grounds, scientists set up small tents and tables displaying their astronomy projects. Not all of the entrants were astronomers, but scientists of all kinds had conducted astronomy experiments to participate in the fair.

There were experiments about the distance of other planets from Earth, the size of stars, space travel, communicating with extraterrestrials, satellites, and much more! The participants had until noon to set up their display. Then, the queen, king, and Sir Hubbard would walk through the fair to find the winner.

Usually, the winner receives a large sum of money and a plaque to hang on their wall. This year, the winner would receive the prizes *and* an invitation to become Trindleview's new royal astronomer!

At noon a trumpet call sounded, and the fair was officially open. The fair was one of the biggest events all year in the kingdom. In addition to the science projects, there were food and craft vendors, musicians and acrobats, and science displays not entered into the contest.

The fair lasted for three days and was visited by thousands of people. The morning sunshine and joyous atmosphere had the queen feeling more positive they would find someone to take Sir Hubbard's place.

The king and queen walked from stall to stall, but so far nothing seemed innovative and exciting enough to win. After an hour, the queen began to feel gloomy again.

The king encouraged her to maintain hope. "We still have many experiments left to see and surely one of them will impress you!" He said.

The queen nodded and continued to walk through the fair, but she had lost interest. Was there no one with an exciting discovery?

As they rounded the corner, the queen noticed a small green tent tucked into a corner. The display was small, and unlike many of the others, there were no flashy colors or gigantic props.

Inside the tent sat a young woman, the queen guessed she could be no more than 20. On her table sat a model of the moon and a simple display board. The queen was intrigued.

Chapter Five

The queen entered the tent and the young woman stood and curtseyed.

The queen examined the display and then gasped. "You believe there is water on the moon?" She said.

"Yes, your majesty," the woman replied. "I know it seems strange or even impossible, but my father studied the moon and so I have been studying the moon all my life. My experiments and observations lead me to believe there is water or ice on the moon."

"Fascinating!" Said the queen. "Hubbard, is this something you've thought too?"

"It has crossed my mind," Hubbard replied, "but it was never my area of expertise."

The queen was encouraged by Hubbard's comments. She asked the young woman to tell her more. Over the next hour, the young astronomer told the queen everything she knew about the moon and why she thought it had polar ice caps like Earth.

She talked about loving the moon since she was a young girl, and how her father had taught her to use a telescope, map the moon's progression in the sky, and predict a lunar eclipse.

After the discussion, the queen felt refreshed. She told the king, on their walk back to the palace, that she believed this young woman should be the next royal astronomer. The king was hesitant at first because she was so young, but once the queen reminded him of everything the woman already knew, he agreed with his wife.

The king and queen observed the remainder of the experiments over the next two days but did not find anything that impressed them more than the young astronomer and her predictions about the moon.

At the end of the fair, the king and queen announced the winner. The queen went personally to the young woman and invited her to the top of the astronomer's tower. At the top of the tower, on the third night of the science fair, the queen asked the young woman to become the royal astronomer.

The woman was amazed. She never thought such a thing could happen! She lived on an island not far from the kingdom and had admired the beautiful astronomer's tower all her life. She could hardly believe it would now be her place of work.

The young woman accepted and thanked the queen many times. The queen left her new royal astronomer in the tower to settle in and slowly walked down the stairs. She felt confident she had found the right person, and while she would always miss Sir Hubbard, he was right, change could be a good thing.

Reading Comprehension Questions for:
The Astronomer's Tower:

1. What did visitors often mistake the astronomer's tower as being? Why?

2. Why did the king and queen need to find a new astronomer?

3. The story says the king and queen wanted to see *innovative* experiments. What do you think *innovative* means?

4. Why was the queen worried the night before the science fair?

5. How did the queen feel at the end of the story? Why?

The Greatest Baseball Player That Ever Lived

Chapter One

If you were to ask some baseball fans who the greatest baseball player that ever lived was, you would probably get a handful of different answers. Baseball is a complicated sport that requires players to be good at both offense and defense. Offense is when you are trying to score, and defense is when you are trying to stop the other team from scoring. Many other sports, like football, soccer, and hockey only require a player to play one position.

However, in baseball, players often switch positions, and they must be able to field and hit the ball. And even though baseball is a two-sided sport, many players who become famous are known for their ability to hit the ball.

For a person who loves baseball, few things are more exciting than watching a game on a beautiful sunny day, especially when your team hits a home run!

In the United States, baseball is known as America's favorite sport and is a popular pastime during spring and summer. Many young kids have played little league hoping they will become the next great player.

Any player who makes it to the major leagues is talented, but what does it take to earn the title of "greatest"? Why do some players go down in history as better than others? Is it luck or skill or a little of both?

Being on the right team at the right time certainly helps. Baseball is a team sport. It takes all nine players working together to win a game. Still, some players stand out and rise to the top. So, what does it take to earn the title of "greatest player"? Let's take a look at some of the top baseball players of all time and then *you* can decide who was the greatest player that ever lived.

Chapter Two

Without a doubt, one of the best baseball players of all time was Willie Mays (born May 6, 1931). Willie Mays was a talented baseball player both offensively and defensively. A star center fielder, he is famous for catching a ball over his shoulder during the eighth inning of a World Series game in 1954. Now that's impressive! He would only win the World Series that one time, but he had many more personal successes within the sport.

Willie Mays won the MVP Award, most valuable player, in 1954 and 1965. And he won the Gold Glove Award, an award given to players who show exceptional skill fielding, 12 years in a row from 1957–1968! This accomplishment alone has led many to say that Willie Mays is the greatest baseball player that ever lived.

And as if his amazing fielding wasn't enough, he also holds sixth place on the list of most career home runs after hitting 660!

The player holding the record for the most home runs, is Willie Mays' godson, Barry Bonds (born July 24, 1964) who hit a career total of 762! However, Barry Bonds was never a fan favorite despite his success on the field. He is accused of using performance-enhancing steroids in the latter part of his career and of lying to a grand jury. The charges were dropped, but many fans lost faith in the slugger. Because of the concerns surrounding Bonds, he was never voted into the Baseball Hall of Fame.

Nonetheless, he often makes the list of the greatest baseball players that have ever played. Barry Bonds won the MVP Award seven times in his career and was selected for the All-Star team

14 times. He has a record of 514 stolen bases: that's a lot of fast running!

Whether or not you agree with the voters' decision to not include Barry Bonds in the Hall of Fame, his hitting record has stood the test of time. He still holds the record for most home runs hit in a single season with 73. The only two people who came close were Ryan Howard and Giancarlo Stanton. Howard, who played for the Philadelphia Phillies, hit 58 home runs in 2006. The following year, Stanton hit 59 playing for the Yankees. Will Bonds' record ever be beaten? We don't know! But his record was set in 2001 and has stood for a long time!

Chapter Three

Many of the players considered to be the greatest of all time are sluggers. They're known for their home runs and powerful bats. No list of great baseball players would be complete without George Ruth (February 6, 1895–August 16, 1948) more famously known as Babe Ruth. He might even be the most famous baseball player who has ever played the game! Even people who are not baseball fans have heard of Babe Ruth.

He is so famous that many argue the popular candy bar, Baby Ruth, is named after him. The powerful slugger himself staked this claim because it came out in 1921 at the height of his career.

However, the candy company that created the bar states it was named after President Grover Cleveland's daughter. In the end, the candy company's story was confirmed, but today many people assume it was named for the famous baseballer and Maryland native.

Babe Ruth holds the third-highest record for career home runs, a whopping 714! He had the second-highest record from 1935 to 1975, for 40 years until Hank Aaron hit his 715th home run in 1975. Currently, Babe Ruth still holds the highest batting average of any player, 0.690. That number means Babe Ruth hit the ball nearly seven out of every ten times at bat. In comparison, most batters sit around a 0.2–0.35 average. Most professional baseball players only hit the ball two or three times out of every ten.

However, despite Ruth's very high batting average, Hank Aaron (February 5, 1934–January 22, 2021) managed to beat Ruth's home run record with a career total of 755! Not only was Hank Aaron an excellent batter, but he was a skilled fielder too.

Aaron played in the outfield and won the Golden Glove Award three times. He also was selected for the All-Star team 21 years in a row. That's nearly his entire baseball career! During Hank Aaron's amazing baseball career, he batted 2,297 runs.

Chapter Four

All of the players mentioned so far have been famous for their power behind the plate, but another name that needs to be on this list is Walter Johnson, a pitcher (November 6, 1887–December 10, 1946). Johnson's nickname was the Big Train, and he is said to have the greatest fastball in history.

During his 21 seasons as a pitcher, he struck out 3,508 batters, a record he held from 1927 until 1983 when three different pitchers broke it in the same year, Nolan Ryan, Steve Carlton, and Gaylord Perry.

Walter Johnson holds the record for shutout wins, a win where the other team does not score any runs, with 110. He also holds the second-place spot for most games won by a pitcher with 417.

Another pitcher who potentially deserves the title of greatest baseball player ever is Roger Clemens (born August 4, 1962). Also known as the Rocket, he earned seven Cy Young Awards (best pitcher of the year), threw 4,672 strikeouts in his career and holds the number three spot.

Clemens won the MVP Award in 1986, just two years after he made it to the major leagues. However, he was another player suspected of taking performance-enhancing steroids, so some argue that he does not deserve a spot on the list of top players.

The third and final pitcher on our list is Cy Young himself (March 29, 1867–November 4, 1955). He holds the record for winning pitcher of most major league games ever with 511 games won. This powerhouse pitcher was nicknamed the Cyclone and stopped going to school after only sixth grade.

In 1956, a year after his death, the Cy Young Award was created to honor the best major league pitcher each year. During his 22-season career, he pitched 7,356 balls. What an arm!

Chapter Five

Many other players could be added to this list and baseball fans have long debated who deserves the title of greatest baseball player who ever lived. Some would argue it was Jackie Robinson (January 13, 1919–October 24, 1972), who was the first African American to play in the MLB. He also became the first African American to win MVP and he won Rookie of the Year in 1947, his first season playing in the MLB.

Other fans may say the best player ever was Honus Wagner, whose baseball card is the most valuable card in history. It's valued at around two million dollars! He led the National League batting average eight times in his career and still ranks among the top 25 for most hits, triples, doubles, and singles.

Others still might argue for Stan Musial (November 21, 1920–January 19, 2013), the St. Louis slugger who led his team the Cardinals to three World Series Wins in 1942, 1944, and 1946.

And many more names could be added to this list, depending on who you ask. Deciding who was the best baseball player, like many sports, isn't a simple issue. There are many things to consider such as when they played, why they are considered good, and what records they set or exceeded.

But no matter how you look at it, some players rise above the rest. And who knows, in another five, ten, or 20 years, there may be new players who are playing now or who haven't started playing yet that will be considered the greatest baseball player that ever lived.

Reading Comprehension Questions for:
The Greatest Baseball Player that Ever Lived:

1. Why was Barry Bonds not voted into the Baseball Hall of Fame? Do you think it was fair? Why or why not?

2. Why is Babe Ruth considered one of the best baseball players?

3. How long did Babe Ruth hold the record for most career home runs? Who beat him and when?

4. What is the Cy Young Award? Why is it called that?

5. Which of the baseball players from the story do you think deserves the title of the best player that ever lived? Why?

The Wizard, The Minstrel, and I

Chapter One

The wizard, the minstrel, and I were the best of friends. We had always been the best of friends for as long as any of us could remember. We were friends long before the wizard was a wizard, long before the minstrel was a minstrel, and long before I became a baker. As toddlers, we played together in our mothers' kitchens. As kids, we ran about the town square causing mischief of one kind and another. And, as teenagers, we each settled into our ways while staying the best of friends.

The wizard moved into the castle to study wizardry from the best wizards in the kingdom. The minstrel, who had always loved music and played the lute, began to study music from one of the most famous musicians in the kingdom. And I began learning how to bake all my mother's wonderful cakes, breads, and pies so that one day I would run her bakery.

You probably think that a wizard, minstrel, and baker being friends is odd. What things could we possibly have in common? But our friendship was so old and true, that even as our interests changed and we grew older, our bond to one another stayed the same.

However, one dark and stormy evening, as many of these tales go, something would happen to test our friendship. By this time, I had been a baker for many years, the wizard was now the chief wizard at the castle, and the minstrel was famous all over the kingdom. We saw one another less than we would have liked, but our friendship remained. I sometimes felt envious of my friends' fame and fortune but never told them.

The night it all started the wizard was advising young magicians, the minstrel was on a tour performing on the other side of the kingdom, and I was in my bakery baking bread.

Chapter Two

A loud crack of thunder sounded from the sky. The thunder was so loud it shook my shop! The wizard, who was deep inside the castle walls, said he also heard the thunder crack. And you may not believe me, but the minstrel said that, even on the far side of the kingdom, the crack was heard.

News of the loud thunder quickly spread throughout the kingdom. It was sudden, and loud, but happened once and only once. The sky was cloudy and dark, but no rain came. When no more thunder sounded, and no rain fell from the sky, people began to question whether it really was thunder.

Who had ever heard of thunder only happening once? Who had ever heard of thunder so loud it could be heard all over the kingdom? People pondered and puzzled over the mysterious thunder for days, but soon it was forgotten.

But, as soon as people began to forget about the thunder, strange things began happening. At first, no one thought much of these strange things. They were small, singular events that people pushed out of their minds as odd but not worrisome. They heard about neighbors quarreling, friends and families breaking apart, items going missing, and some neighbors suddenly becoming wealthy!

As more and more strange events happened and travelers swapped stories in taverns and inns, people began to realize that something odd indeed was happening! Why were so many friends and neighbors fighting?

I did not hear many of these stories as most of my customers were town locals who rarely traveled. I never thought any of these odd events would affect me in my tiny bakery. But this is where I was wrong.

One normal, sunny morning, a strange event happened to me. And this event is what would test my friendship with the wizard and the minstrel. Into my shop walked an elderly woman I had never seen before. She hobbled up to my counter and asked me for two small buns.

She slid the coins across the counter, took her buns, and turned to leave my shop. However, before she left, this is what she said:

I know what you wish, and your wish I can grant.
But there are three things I need from you, or I can't.
You wish to be famous like both of your friends.
If you finish my tasks, I am the means to that end.
If you wish to have a fortune and rise to the top,
The first thing I need is some magical drops.
A red shiny potion that comes in a black bottle.
Next, I'll need a string from the lute of the minstrel.
The last thing I'll need to grant you your wish.
Is a circular, golden, shiny, jeweled dish.
Find me these three by the end of the week.
And I'll grant you your wish, the fame that you seek.
But watch out for the maker of magic and the singer of songs.
Before your quest finishes, they will both do you wrong.

Then she turned and walked out of my shop. I did not know what to think! It was true that I felt jealous of my friends' fame and fortune, but I had never told anyone, so how could she know?

I realized the woman must be a witch. That was the only way she could know my secret wish and be able to grant it!

Chapter Three

I thought over and over of the three objects the witch had requested. She wanted magical red drops from a black bottle, a string from a minstrel's lute, and a shiny, golden, jeweled dish. I thought I would just ask my friend the wizard for the magical drops and the minstrel for the string. The golden dish would be more difficult.

As soon as I closed my bakery for the evening, I walked up the hill toward the castle. I walked around to the side of the castle and knocked on the heavy wooden door. A few minutes later, my friend the wizard opened the door.

He greeted me with a hug and invited me inside. The wizard's den was a magical place! There were animals of all kinds chittering happily in pens and crates, and there were skulls and candles in every color and shape you could imagine. And, on the back wall, there were dozens of bottles, full of potions glistening in the candlelight.

I did not want to ask the wizard for the potion right away, so instead we sat and ate some buns I brought from my bakery while talking. As he told me about his latest students, I examined the potion bottles over his shoulder. I did not see a single black bottle.

"My friend," I said eventually, "I can't help but notice you have bottles of almost every color, but no black!"

"Ah," he said. "The black bottles are used for my most powerful potions, so I keep them locked up. This way a student doesn't accidentally use them."

"Where do you keep them locked? May I see?" I asked.

So, my friend showed me the cabinet where the powerful potions were locked. I saw seven black bottles but was unsure if any had red potion.

"What types of potions are these?" I asked.

The wizard began taking them out one at a time and showing them to me. The fourth bottle he took out he said was a magical youth potion. He allowed me to peek inside, and I saw a bright red color. This was the bottle I needed! But how would I get some? He would think it odd if I asked.

At the moment, luck was on my side. One of his students rushed in and said they needed help with a spell. The wizard apologized to me, asked me to lock up the potions, and dashed out. This was my chance! I slipped the potion bottle into my pocket, locked the cabinet, and hurried back home.

Chapter Four

The next day, my friend the minstrel knocked on my bakery door. He was home from his tour! I greeted him and asked him to sit and talk with me. I watched as he sat his lute in the corner. I eyed the strings. I needed one of them, but could I just ask? No, he would think it was odd I wanted a string and might not give it to me.

My friend told me tales of his travels and how glad he was to be home at last. He pointed to his lute and told me it needed some repairs. He needed to take it to the music shop down the street, but he was so tired and wanted to sleep.

I realized this was my chance to get a string. "I will take it to the shop for you; you go home and rest," I said.

"Oh, thank you, my friend," the minstrel replied. "I am so grateful for I really need to rest!"

I gave my friend a pat on the back, sent him on his way home, and once he was out of sight, removed one of the strings from the lute. I then did as I promised and took the lute to the music shop.

I now had two of the three items! But where would I find a golden and jeweled dish?

I was in bed that night worrying about where I would find the dish when I heard a loud crash outside my shop.

I ran down the stairs and saw a merchant's cart with a broken wheel. Many of his goods had fallen off his wagon and were scattered about. I was beginning to help him clean up when I noticed a golden dish that had rolled behind a barrel. I let the dish sit there, helped the driver fix his wheel, and sent him on his way. Now I had all three items!

The witch was due to return in two days, and I could not wait to have my wish of fame and fortune granted!

Chapter Five

The day before the witch was going to return, there came a knock at my door. It was the castle guards! The guards told me I was under arrest for stealing one of the wizard's powerful potions and stealing a string from the minstrel's lute. I could not believe it; my friends had betrayed me!

The guards led me up the hill to the castle jail and placed me in a cell.

The wizard came to visit me and said, "My friend, I do not know why you stole from me, but if you had only asked, I would have shared my potion with you!"

I realized then that my friend hadn't betrayed me. I had betrayed my friend by not trusting him and stealing from him. I felt ashamed.

Shortly after the wizard left, the minstrel came to visit. He asked why I pretended I wanted to help so I could steal a string from his lute. "I have so many strings!" he said. "If you had asked, I would have gladly given you one."

Again, I felt the shame of stealing from my friend and not trusting him. I was so blinded by my wish I did not think of my friends.

The wizard and the minstrel forgave me and allowed me to return to my bakery. I apologized many times and said I understood if they no longer wanted to be my friend. Both my friends said everyone makes mistakes, but that it may be hard to trust me in the future.

Back at my shop, the merchant with the broken wheel stopped by. He asked if I had seen the golden dish, he lost last night. I said yes, and that I was ashamed I had stolen it because I needed it.

The merchant said I could keep the dish as thanks for helping him in the middle of the night, but he wished I had asked him instead of taking it. I apologized and gave him his dish and said I was too ashamed to keep it.

When the witch returned, I told her what had happened and she said, "You see? I told you your friends would betray you!"

"No, you are wrong," I replied. "I betrayed my friends by not trusting them enough to help me. I no longer wish to have fame and fortune. I see now that friendship is more important than those things."

The witch cursed and stomped her foot and was very angry, but I refused to help her again. With a loud bang that shook my walls like an earthquake, the witch disappeared. I realized she was the cause of the loud bang and the odd happenings. She must have been going from town to town, tricking people into helping her and I had broken the spell by refusing to help her.

I knew now that I may not have money and fame like my two best friends, but I have their friendship and that is the most valuable thing of all!

Reading Comprehension Questions for:
The Wizard, The Minstrel, and I:

1. How long have the baker, the wizard, and the minstrel been friends?

2. What was it about his friends that made the baker jealous?

3. What did the baker realize about friendship at the end of the story?

4. Do you think the wizard and minstrel were right to forgive the baker? Why or why not?

Maisey the Magnificent Cat

Chapter One

If you walk through the town and down the side road you will see a small white cottage with blue shutters. And in the window of this cottage there usually sits a black and white cat. To anyone walking by the cottage, this cat looks like an ordinary cat. She has no special markings, she isn't too big or too small, and she has four average-sized paws and a regular cat tail. This cat often lies in the sun, like cats do, sleeping with a drowsy look on her face. Yes, all in all, this cat looks like an ordinary cat.

But this cat is, in fact, *not* an ordinary cat. This cat is Maisey. And Maisey is a magnificent cat. Maisey is magnificent for many reasons, but you probably won't believe them even if you know what they were! That's because no one has ever seen all the wonderful things Maisey can do.

Cats are mysterious creatures, and Maisey, like all other cats, has a secret side her owners never see. Now, most cats' secret side is to do simple things like sneaking off into the night to hunt for mice or frogs. Or, knowing the perfect way to tease the dog without getting caught.

Most people think cats are lazy, but that's only what cats want you to think. If people think cats are lazy and sit and sleep in the sun all day, then it is easier for a cat's secret side to exist.

Cats have lived with humans for thousands of years and no human has truly discovered a cat's secret side, though a few have come close. The Egyptians worshipped cats as gods; perhaps because one day a pharaoh caught a cat doing something extraordinary!

The Greeks worshipped cats too; they believed the goddess Hecate could turn into a cat. She was the goddess of the hunt; something cats are very good at! The Norse also worshipped a cat as the goddess of magic.

These ancient cultures must have known something about cats that we've forgotten, either that or cats have become better at hiding their secret side - or, for most cats, the secret side has become less amazing. Whatever the case, Maisey was a magnificent cat, and her secret side was more amazing than your average kitty!

Chapter Two

Maisey loved her home. The family she lived with was kind and loving and the cottage was cozy and the windowsill warm and sunny. She had no complaints at all other than sometimes she became bored. There were birds and squirrels to chase outside and mice to hunt in the basement and the attic. The family gave her toys and played with her and scratched behind her ears the way she liked. But there was not much adventure in the cozy cottage.

So, sometimes, Maisey had to go out and find adventure. One of the things that made Maisey so magnificent was her speed. She was the fastest cat around.

At night, when the family was asleep, she would dash out her cat door, into the woods, and seek adventure.

She loved to climb the tallest trees and leap from limb to limb. If anyone saw her, they would think she was a small mountain lion, not a regular house cat!

She leaped through the air with a grace unknown to other cats. Why, it almost looked like she was flying! And perhaps she was - Maisey was indeed a magnificent cat with special hidden talents.

One night while Maisey was prowling and jumping through the woods she met another cat. This cat was bigger than Maisey. He was almost completely white except he had dark circles around his eyes that looked like eyeglasses. He was perched upon a branch high in a tree when Maisey landed with an almost silent thud.

The cat, half hidden in the shadows, said, "I've been watching you. You are quite a magnificent cat."

"Why, thank you," said Maisey, "but why have you been watching me?"

"I am Horatio," said the big cat, "and I am in charge of a secret society for the most amazing cats. I believe you belong in our group!"

Maisey was shocked. "A secret cat society?"

"Yes," replied Horatio. "It has been around for thousands of years. But, only the most marvelous cats are invited to join. I've seen how you jump and leap, almost like you are flying. That is a special skill. Meet me here tomorrow at 10 p.m. and I will take you to the first meeting."

Maisey thought for a moment. "Alright," she said.

"Wonderful!" Horatio replied. "Until then, goodnight!" And he jumped out of the tree and padded into the forest.

Maisey was intrigued; she had never heard of such a group. Did she really belong? The only way to find out was to return for the meeting tomorrow night. And that's exactly what Maisey decided to do.

Chapter Three

All day Maisey thought about the secret cat meeting. However, anyone watching Maisey that day would have no idea what she was thinking or that she was thinking at all. Cats are not like dogs who show all their emotions on their faces. Cats always look bored or uninterested; that is how they keep secrets so well.

Maisey did all the normal things she usually did during the day. She sat on the windowsill and enjoyed the sunlight. She played with her owners and chased a toy mouse around the living room floor. And she meowed loudly when it was time for her dinner. Once her owners had settled in for the night watching a movie, she knew she could sneak away, and she did.

Using all her stealth and speed, she ran through the grass and then jumped from tree to tree. Within minutes she was back at the spot where she met Horatio the night before. He was already there waiting for her.

Without much more than a nod, he said, "Good evening, please follow me."

Maisey followed Horatio out of the tree and through the woods. He was not fast like Maisey, at least he didn't seem to be. Maisey wondered what his secret skills were. After several minutes of walking, they reached a large tree with a hole in the bottom of the trunk.

"We're here," Horatio told her. "Welcome to the Society of Magnificent Cats!" He said and led her into the hollow trunk.

Inside the tree, a path led down in a circular direction. When they reached the bottom, the space opened up into a huge cavern.

What Maisey saw amazed her. There were cats everywhere! Cats of every size, shape, and color doing the most magnificent things!

Horatio's eyes sparkled as he watched Maisey. He always loved seeing a cat's first reaction to this sight. "Walk around and enjoy yourself!" He told her and off he went.

Chapter Four

Now if you were impressed with Maisey's ability to swiftly run and jump, then you'd be amazed by the cats you saw here. There were cats juggling and dancing. A cat was walking along a tightrope. Maisey even saw one cat flying on a trapeze! It was like a circus.

But as she went further into the cavern, she saw that not all the astounding cats were performing physical acts. She saw cats reading books in a small library. Maisey did not realize that cats *could* read, although she had never tried. She saw cats knitting and sewing. And she saw cats playing musical instruments.

Maisey had no idea there were so many magnificent cats! She walked around in awe wondering if she could learn to do any of these things.

Horatio found her and asked, "Are you impressed?"

"Oh yes!" Said Maisey. "I've been so lonely and bored because I did not know there were so many amazing cats. Most of the cats I know are intelligent but do not wish for adventure and fun like this!"

"We meet once a week and share our secret talents. You can learn as many as you'd like!" Horatio told her.

Maisey was excited. Over the following months, Maisey learned to read and tap dance. She learned how to juggle and play the piano. Maisey taught others how to run and jump silently and how to appear like they were flying through the sky.

Maisey could only practice her talents when her human family was asleep or away. But once in a while they would come home and wonder why a book had fallen off the shelf, or think to themselves, "Didn't I put the piano lid down earlier?" Once, Maisey's owner thought he saw her juggling toy mice out of the corner of his eye, but when he turned, he saw her sitting on the floor batting the toy between her paws.

How silly, he thought. *Cats can't juggle!*

Maisey was a truly magnificent cat, only no one would believe it, even if you told them!

Reading Comprehension Questions for:
Maisey the Magnificent Cat

1. Which ancient cultures worshipped cats? What did they believe?

2. The story says Maisey was *intrigued* by the secret cat group. What do you think the word *intrigued* means?

3. Where was the Secret Society of Magnificent Cats hidden? How did Maisey get there?

4. There are a lot of words used in the story that mean magnificent. Make a list of all the synonyms (words with the same meaning) for magnificent used.

5. What secret talents did Maisey learn from the other cats? What did her owner almost catch her doing one time?

From Sea to Shining Sea - Traveling Route 66

Chapter One

"That's everything!" Ryan's dad yelled, closing the trunk of the car. A minute later, the rest of Ryan's family came through the open front door and climbed into the RV his parents had rented for their family vacation. Ryan's family was going to drive across the county along the famous Route 66.

Ryan was not excited about this vacation. He wanted to do something fun like scuba diving in Florida like they did last year or skiing in Denver the year before. Driving across the country with his dad, mom, and sister did not sound fun. His parents seemed really excited though, and he couldn't understand why. How was driving along a long road fun?

Ryan lived in Skokie, Illinois and Route 66 began a few miles south of his town in Chicago. Once they drove out of Chicago, his mom said they would make their first stop in Springfield, IL, where Abraham Lincoln was born. His mom had made a big map and marked all the spots they would stop at along the way.

Ryan was excited about seeing Los Angeles and the Pacific Ocean but that wouldn't happen until the end of the trip. He had asked a few weeks ago why they couldn't just fly to L.A. and vacation there. His dad said because it was all about the American Experience and learning some of the history of the country. History was Ryan's least favorite class.

Chapter Two

It had only been three hours but to Ryan, it felt like an eternity. He tried to read his mystery book but couldn't concentrate because his parents kept pointing out things through the window.

Will the whole trip be like this? He wondered.

After another 20 minutes, his dad parked the RV in front of a large cream-colored building.

"Stop number one!" His dad called out. "The Lincoln Library and Museum."

"Great," Ryan muttered, stepping down from the back of the RV. He wasn't excited about the museum but it did feel good to stretch his legs, though, and he did like libraries.

Once inside, his dad said, "OK everyone, you have 90 minutes to see whatever you want! Meet back here at 1:30!"

Ryan's family went off in different directions.

What am I going to do for 90 minutes? Ryan thought. He trudged toward an exhibit about Lincoln's youth. As Ryan walked through the exhibit, he started to read the exhibit signs and became interested.

When he thought of Lincoln, he usually just thought of a tall funny-looking man in a hat. He had no idea Lincoln had done so many interesting things *before* becoming president.

Ryan went from exhibit to exhibit and before he knew it, his 90 minutes were up. He met his family at the entrance, and they piled back into the RV for the next part of the journey.

Their next stop was only an hour away in Litchfield, IL. Ryan wondered why they were stopping so soon. They visited a local museum and a farmer's market. Then his dad checked them into a hotel for the night. Ryan thought it was odd they were only driving four hours the first day, but when night came, he understood why.

His dad drove the RV to a giant outdoor movie theater where they ordered dinner and watched a movie sitting in front of the RV on camper chairs. Ryan had heard of these old-fashioned drive-in theaters but didn't know they still existed.

"This is pretty cool," he said to his parents and they both smiled.

Chapter Three

Over the next few days, Ryan's family stopped at several places along Route 66. First was Livingston, IL with the Pink Elephant antique diner where they ate breakfast the first morning. Then they drove over the Mississippi River on the Old Chain of Rocks Bridge and entered the city of St. Louis. They spent an entire day in St. Louis and rode to the top of the famous Gateway Arch.

Ryan thought the views were amazing! He felt like a bird perched on top of a tall building. Before they left the city, they went to the St. Louis Car Museum. This was Ryan's favorite thing yet! He had never seen so many colorful and cool old-fashioned cars. He pulled his dad from one car to the next, pointing out the chrome wheels, the fancy headlights, the brightly colored detailing, or the silver engines sparkling in the light.

Their next stop was even better. They visited the Meramec Caverns. He had never seen anything like these underground caverns. In fact, he hadn't even known caverns existed! Walking through these ancient stone caverns was like entering an underground and magical world of trolls. It was amazing that nature could create something so spectacular completely underground.

After leaving the caverns, they continued to travel through Missouri, stopping at old-fashioned gas stations, admiring old bridges, and viewing beautiful murals. At the end of two days, they had crossed Missouri and were entering Kansas. After Kansas, they entered Oklahoma.

By the time they entered Oklahoma, Ryan was no longer bored in the RV. He enjoyed looking out the window and finding strange giant statues with his sister. They even saw one that was a giant blue whale! Visiting the old-fashioned gas stations felt like stepping back in time and he loved the neon signs that lit up attractions and restaurants as day turned into night.

At each stop, Ryan learned a little more about his country's history and was beginning to think history wasn't so boring after all. When they reached Oklahoma City, Ryan was looking forward to their next stop, the National Cowboy and Western Heritage Museum.

Chapter Four

Walking through the cowboy museum was like being transported even further back in time than driving along Route 66. Ryan thought the old-fashioned fake town was like a movie set. He wanted to pretend he was an Old West cowboy, or at least an actor playing one!

With the old-fashioned storefronts and train depot, it was easy to imagine. He wondered what it was truly like to live in the Old West. It was probably pretty dangerous. Survival was probably difficult, and there wasn't a grocery store or mall you could just visit when you needed things.

As Ryan's family continued their travels through Oklahoma, he learned a lot about Native Americans. Their culture and history were fascinating in a different way from the American history he knew. After all, Native American history *was* American history! The way they valued nature and the earth was so different from most people he knew. He respected the Native Americans and made a promise to himself that he would learn more!

One of the biggest parts of the trip was traveling through Texas. And perhaps the strangest thing on the entire trip was the Cadillac Ranch! At the Cadillac Ranch, there was a row of graffitied Cadillacs half buried in the ground. It was a strange monument. Ryan saw one man using spray paint to add to one of the cars.

"People bring spray paint to add their mark to the cars," his dad told him. "But it doesn't stay long because so many visitors do the same!"

Ryan thought ever-changing art was a cool idea, and he wondered where else in the world there was something similar. He never realized so many strange and wonderful things existed in his country.

After Texas, his family drove their RV into New Mexico. Ryan instantly fell in love with New Mexico's landscape and architecture. The sand-colored buildings were so different from anything they had in Illinois. The city of Santa Fe was as if an old-fashioned town and a modern city had molded together. The mountains in the background were colorful in shades of red, orange, and pink that matched the sunset.

And as Ryan thought about Illinois, it felt like it had been months since they'd left home - when it had actually only been two weeks! He couldn't believe how much he had seen and done in only two weeks.

His family spent the night in Santa Fe, and the following day and then began traveling toward Arizona. Arizona was the state for natural wonders! Here they saw a giant crater in the ground that looked like it belonged on the moon and eventually, they came to the greatest wonder of all, the Grand Canyon.

The Grand Canyon took Ryan's breath away. The caverns back in Missouri had been amazing, but the Grand Canyon was amazing times by ten! He stood and looked for the longest time taking in the peaks and valleys created by nature.

He knew tomorrow his family would enter California and there were only three days left in his vacation. From California, they would fly home to Illinois. He thought about how he hadn't wanted to go on this vacation and was sure it would be boring, but it had been the exact opposite. He never would have known all these amazing places existed or that there was so much interesting history!

Ryan was sad his trip was coming to an end but grateful for the experience. He couldn't wait to see the Pacific Ocean but was so glad he had stopped to see everything along the way.

Reading Comprehension Questions for:
From Sea to Shining Sea - Traveling Route 66

1. How did Ryan feel about his family vacation at the beginning of the trip? Why did he feel that way?

2. When did Ryan start to change his mind about the trip? What happened?

3. List some of the places Ryan's family stopped and some of the things they saw.

4. How did Ryan's feelings change from the beginning of the trip to the end? Why did they change?

Lost in the Library

Chapter One

Dawn was just peeking over the horizon when Margo reached the library. The early morning hours, just before the sun broke into the sky was her favorite time of day. There was peacefulness and quietness in the early morning before everyone woke up and added their noise to the day. She enjoyed the calm and quiet because it allowed her to think. She found the sound of cars driving, loud bus brakes, and people chattering distracting. That is why Margo loved working in the library; it was nearly always quiet.

There was the occasional loud noise, someone dropping a book or a child squealing, but usually, the library was quiet. After all, silence in the library was the one rule everyone knew! And when people did need to speak, it was always done in hushed voices just above a whisper unless you were in the children's area. But the children's area was down a hall and behind a set of heavy glass doors and the noise didn't carry to the main library.

Margo was glad children enjoyed coming to the library, but she was even more glad they had a special area to play and be loud that didn't interrupt the peace and calm of the place.

Margo slipped the library key into the door and entered the main hall. The moment she stepped inside, she was hit with the smell of books. She loved the smell of books more than any other smell in the world. Books smelt like history and adventure. They smelt like far-off places and dreams.

Margo hung her sweater on the back of her chair and began her morning walk around the library. She liked to spend time each morning walking through the shelves and enjoying the quiet of the empty library.

Soon her co-workers would arrive and then the library patrons. And while the library was never loud, the silence of being alone among all the books was unique.

Chapter Two

Margo did not have a set path she took. Each morning she would walk whichever way felt right and simply follow her impulses. She wasn't looking for anything or trying to complete a task, she only wanted to walk around the library and enjoy the quiet.

She flipped on the electric tea kettle that was set on her desk so that when her walk was finished, she could pour a hot cup of tea to enjoy. Today Margo turned to her left and entered the fiction section. Margo loved reading all types of books, but fiction, especially adventure books, was her favorite. *Treasure Island*, *Alice in Wonderland*, and *Harry Potter* were among her favorite books.

The shelves in the fiction section were tall, twice as tall as she was. To reach books at the top you needed to use a special rolling ladder. Being amongst the tall bookstacks made her feel as if she were lost in a maze of books.

As Margo walked through the fiction section, she replaced any books that were lying around, straightened the shelves, and stayed on the lookout for a title she hadn't noticed before. As she reached the end of the second row, she noticed a red and gold book sitting on the end of the shelf.

The book had a deep red cover and gold embossed letters along the spine. She had never noticed this book before, which she thought was odd because it stood out from the other, duller books nearby. *Perhaps it is mis-shelved*, she thought.

As she neared the book, she read the spine: *The Hidden Stacks* by Dirgel Awdur. *What an odd name,* she thought. She had never heard of this author before. It appeared to be misplaced because it was sitting in the middle of the "C" section right next to Lewis Carrol and one of Margo's favorites, *Alice in Wonderland.*

Margo reached up to move the book so she could return it to the correct spot, but the book wouldn't move. She tugged harder and as she did, the book fell into her hands. At the same time, in the center of the floor, she noticed a circular motion. The floorboards were spinning! As they spun, they opened to reveal a stone staircase leading down.

Margo peered down the stairwell and called, "Hello!" but no one answered. "Well, this is certainly an adventure," she said out loud and stepped down onto the first stair. She had no idea how this mysterious staircase came to be in the library, but she was ready to explore!

Chapter Three

Margo didn't feel scared but wondered if perhaps she should. She was in the library, after all, a perfectly safe place. But she had read enough adventure stories to know that mysterious stairwells might lead anywhere! Perhaps there was pirate treasure buried beneath the library, or a dragon sleeping in a cave! Better yet, maybe it was the entry way to a magic kingdom like Alice found when she fell down the rabbit hole.

No matter what she found, Margo was sure it would be an adventure. She slowly climbed down the stairs, and it became darker as she went. "Perhaps I should have grabbed a flashlight," she said aloud. But as soon as she said the words, torches lit up along the stairwell. "That works!" She said.

Seeing clearly, she walked more quickly down the stairs. When she reached the bottom, she entered a small cavern that led off into three different tunnels. *A good adventure always gives the hero choices*, she thought. "One, two, or three," she said out loud. As she said each number, each tunnel lit up with a different color.

The first tunnel had a pale pink light, the second tunnel shone green, and the third was a golden yellow. Margo chose the golden yellow tunnel. She wasn't sure why, but something pulled her in that direction.

Chapter Four

Margo followed the golden-yellow light, and it grew brighter with each step. When she reached the end of the tunnel, she was in a room filled with books. *Why, it's another library!* She looked up and saw a sign that read *The Library of Lost Books*. She repeated the name out loud and then began wandering through the shelves. She read the titles and did not see a single book she recognized.

"I wonder why these books are lost?" She said.

With a soft pop, a small man with a long white beard wearing a golden suit appeared next to her.

"They are lost because once they were written the manuscripts were never published and were lost," said the man.

"Oh, hello," said Margo. "You must be the librarian."

"I am," replied the man. "I am Atticus, at your service. Now that you have found your way to the Library of Lost Books, you are welcome to borrow any book you like!"

Margo was delighted. "What about the other two tunnels? Are those libraries as well?"

"They are," replied Atticus, "but I cannot tell you what you will find, for each person who finds their way down here discovers different libraries. The only way for you to know is to enter them yourself."

Margo thanked Atticus and asked her how she would find his library again.

"Now that you know it is here, you will find it any time you need it."

Margo selected a book from the shelf and signed it out by writing her name in a large golden book sitting near the entrance. Then, she exited the Library of Lost Books and walked back into the cavern.

She decided to visit the other libraries in order. Next, she went to the one in the middle, the green one. She entered the green library with a bit more excitement and less fear since she knew books were waiting for her at the end of the tunnel. When she entered the room, she saw words spiraling all over the walls like snakes. At least she thought they were words; she couldn't make sense of anything they said.

The sign above this door read *The Library of Lost Languages*. Now Margo understood why she couldn't read anything; all the words were in foreign languages. She walked around looking at books, taking them gently off the shelf to look. She couldn't read any of them but was fascinated by all the languages she saw.

She did not see a librarian here but chose a book to borrow. Perhaps when she took the book back up to her world, she would be able to read it. If not, she would enjoy trying to figure out the story by looking at the illustrations.

The final tunnel, the pink one, was the largest room yet. It looked like the shelves went on for miles. Above her, the sign read, *The Library of Forgotten Books*.

"Oh, how sad," Margo said. "No book should be forgotten." And with this, Margo had an idea. Each week she would come down to the Library of Forgotten Books and choose one to read. Then she would promote the book in the library in hopes people would discover it again!

She spent what felt like hours lost among the shelves of forgotten books until she selected a title, *Mrs. Winkle and the Blueberry Bush* by S. A. Welles.

Margo carried her three books back up the circular stairwell and entered her library again. When she came back to the front desk, her co-worker Sam was there.

"Where have you been?" He asked. "I looked all over the library and couldn't find you."

"Oh," said Margo, shrugging. "I got lost in the library for a bit."

"Right," said Sam. "Well, welcome back," he laughed.

"Thanks," said Margo, already thinking of next week when she would get lost in the library again.

Reading Comprehension Questions for:
Lost in the Library:

1. What did Margo like about the early morning? Why?

2. What book does Margo notice on her morning walk? Why does she notice it?

3. What were the three libraries Margo found? What types of books were in each one?

4. What is Margo's plan for the hidden library she found?

5. Why do you think the story is called *Lost in the Library*?

The Upside-Down World

Chapter One

Jose lived an ordinary life. He had ordinary brown hair and ordinary brown eyes. He lived in an ordinary house with three bedrooms, two bathrooms, and a backyard. His backyard had two ordinary trees, a rose bush with pink roses, an old playset he rarely used anymore, and a shed where his parents kept the lawn equipment.

His house was an ordinary shade of yellow, with a blue front door, blue shutters, and a garden out front. Every morning he woke up, ate an ordinary breakfast of cereal and orange juice, then rode the bus to his ordinary school.

Jose liked his ordinary life. He liked his brown hair and brown eyes. He liked his yellow house with its blue door and pretty garden in the front. He liked playing baseball and football in the backyard with his dad and his friends.

Everything about Jose's life was ordinary, and that was OK with him. He was happy and content. But something very unordinary was about to happen to Jose. But Jose didn't know that yet.

One very ordinary morning when the sun was shining with a few clouds in the sky, the temperature was a comfortable 68 degrees, and he heard birds chirping in the trees, Jose decided to go for a walk.

As Jose walked through the neighborhood, he noticed a rainbow in the distance. *That's odd*, he thought. Rainbows usually only came after rain, and it hadn't rained all week. Jose decided to follow the rainbow and see where it started.

He began walking through the neighborhood, turning left and right. He was not paying attention to where he was walking. He was only focused on following the rainbow.

Finally, Jose stopped walking and realized that he did not know where he was. He did not recognize any of the houses around him or the street names. "Where am I?" He wondered. But then he saw the rainbow again and thought he couldn't be that far from his house. It only felt like he'd been walking for 15 or 20 minutes.

So, Jose continued to follow the rainbow until he discovered where it ended.

Chapter Two

When Jose found the end of the rainbow, it appeared to be in the chimney of a house. This house, unlike Jose's, was not ordinary. In fact, this house seemed put together at odd angles and had odd shapes. The chimney where the rainbow seemed to be entering, was on the side of the house. And now that Jose looked closer, so was the roof.

Jose didn't see a door. *That's odd,* he thought. *How do they get inside?* He noticed the windows were shaped like triangles and the glass in the windows was purple, not clear.

"This is a very odd house," Jose said out loud. Then he noticed the garden. It was completely upside-down and floating in the air! He saw the roots of all the plants and flowers growing upward toward the sky and the blooms were floating just above the ground.

Jose rubbed his eyes. "I must be dreaming," he said to himself.

He looked at the house again. He noticed that it wasn't made from vinyl siding like his house. Nor was it made from bricks like his neighbor's house. It wasn't even wooden like his Aunt Maria's cottage on the beach. This house seemed to be made up of a little bit of everything. Materials and colors were all mixed up together. Nothing he saw made sense. But when he looked around at the other houses on the street, they all appeared ordinary like his.

Jose was staring at this mixed-up house, trying to decide what to make of it, when all of a sudden, a small man popped up through what would be the roof of an ordinary house.

Chapter Three

The small man looked down at Jose and called, "Hello! Nice to meet you! I love it when I have visitors!"

Jose stared. The man was short, almost the same height as him. He had a bright red beard, and he was dressed in a pair of green pants, with a white shirt and a gray vest.

On his head, he had a small green cap that covered more bright red hair.

"What's the matter?" The man said. "Cat got your tongue?"

"Oh, I apologize," Jose said. "I've just never seen anyone climb out of their roof before!"

"My roof?" The man said, confused. "This isn't my roof; this is my front door! My roof is over there," he said, pointing to where the rainbow met the chimney.

"My goodness," Jose said. "Your house is very different from my house."

"I hear that a lot," the man said with a chuckle. "Would you like to come in and have some cookies and milk? I just baked them!"

Jose knew that he was not supposed to enter a stranger's house, but his curiosity overcame him, and he accepted the stranger's invitation.

"How do I get to your front door?" Jose asked the small man.

"Like this!" The stranger said, and a pair of multi-colored stairs appeared descending down the front of the house.

Jose climbed up the stairs and entered the house. As soon as he stepped inside, he said, "Whoa!"

Everything inside the small man's house was upside-down.

Chapter Four

"Your house is upside-down!" Jose said. The small man looked around and thought everything looked ordinary to him. "But we're walking on the ceiling!" Jose exclaimed.

"Where I come from everyone walks on the ceiling. It's your world that seems upside-down to me!" The man said.

The man invited Jose to sit down and then offered him cookies and milk. Jose was amazed that even though the plate was upside-down the cookies didn't fall off. As he sipped his milk, he expected it to dribble out of the cup and spill down his shirt but even the milk seemed to obey the reverse laws of gravity inside this house.

The cookies were warm, sugary, and delicious.

Jose looked at the small man and asked, "Where are you from?"

"Oh, I am from a faraway place with a name most people from your world can't pronounce. However, those who do know of my world call it the Upside-Down World because, to them, everything appears to be topsy-turvy."

"But how did you get here?" Jose asked. "And why did you come here?"

"I traveled along the rainbow to arrive, and I am here because I am the emissary between the two worlds. My house is the entryway to the other world. In fact, only very special people can follow the rainbow and find my house. That is why I invited you in!"

"Me? Special?" No, I am very ordinary indeed," Jose protested.

"Impossible!" The small man said. "Everyone can see the rainbow, but only special people can see my house."

"Why isn't your house upside-down on the outside? It looks all mixed up," Jose asked.

"The magic of my world and your world meet on the outside of my house. So, instead of everything being upside-down, it gets mixed around. Sometimes my door is up high like you saw it, and other times it's underground or even sideways!"

"Fascinating!" Jose said. "I would love to see your world. I feel like I am dreaming right now!"

"I would be happy to show you, my world. But you can only stay a short time, or you will become upside-down yourself!"

And with that, the small man led Jose to a golden, arched doorway at the back of the house.

Chapter Five

The small man opened the door for Jose and handed him a large, golden pocket watch. He told Jose he had one hour to explore but he needed to be back at the golden door in exactly one hour or he would become upside-down forever!

Jose thanked the man and stepped through the door. Because Jose was already upside-down, it didn't seem odd at first. But as he walked, he noticed the trees were growing upside-down and the birds were flying at his feet.

"What a strange place," Jose said to himself.

When he first walked through the door, he was in a grassy field, but as he walked toward the edge of the field, he noticed a small village. He walked, upside-down, following the path to the village.

In the village all the houses were upside-down, and so were the shops. He saw a woman riding a bicycle upside-down with only air beneath her tires! In the center of the village, there was a large, stone fountain that seemed to float upside-down. The water poured out of the fountain toward the ground and then back into the basin without a drop being spilled.

People waved to Jose and smiled, and he waved and smiled back at them. When he noticed he only had 15 minutes left, he hurried out of the village and back toward the golden door. The small man met him there and asked, "What did you think?"

"It was very unlike my ordinary town and everything I am used to, but I rather enjoyed experiencing something out of the ordinary!" Jose replied.

"You are welcome back, anytime!" The small man said. "Anytime you want to visit, just look for the rainbow in the sky!"

Jose thanked the small man and climbed out of his house and down the multi-colored stairs. As he began walking away, he wondered if it had all been a dream.

It didn't feel like a dream. But the only way Jose would know for sure was to look for the rainbow again. So, he turned around and saw the brightly colored rainbow arching through the sky.

"Excuse me," he said to a man walking a dog, "but do you see that rainbow over there?"

"Yes," said the man, "it's quite lovely. And it ends just in that empty lot right there." The man pointed to the spot where the small man's house was.

Jose could see the house, but it seemed the man couldn't.

"Well, have a lovely day!" Jose said to the man and the dog and continued to walk home.

Reading Comprehension Questions for:
The Upside-Down World

1. How did Jose feel about his ordinary life?

2. How did Jose end up at the mixed-up house?

3. Based on the small man's description and the fact that a rainbow is connected to his house, who or what do you think he is?

4. The small man asks Jose if a *cat has got his tongue.* What do you think this expression means? Why?

5. Jose accepted the invitation from the man to enter his house. This is a fictional story. In real life, should you ever enter a stranger's house without a parent or trusted adult? Why or why not?

6. Jose mentions several times that he thinks he must be dreaming. Do you think he is dreaming? Why or why not?

Race to the Sky - The Chrysler and Empire State Buildings

Chapter One

The New York City skyline is famous. People from around the world recognize NYC and part of that recognition is because it has two very famous buildings, the Chrysler Building and the Empire State Building. Finished less than a year apart, they each held the title of World's Tallest Building.

The United States had a very fast-growing economy in the 1920s, which eventually led to the stock market crash of 1929 and an era known as The Great Depression. But before the stock market crash was a decade known as the Roaring Twenties. It was a period of big business, big construction, and big parties.

The American people were celebrating their victory in World War I. In a booming economy, people bought cars, took vacations, flew on the new commercial airlines, and witnessed many big construction projects.

Everyone wanted the biggest and the best and the same went for the country's biggest city. New York wanted to have the biggest buildings. And in the mid-1920s, architect William Van Alen was hired to do just that!

The original plan for the Chrysler Building was 40 stories. It was going to be the new headquarters for the car company Chrysler Corporation. But as planning continued, the building grew taller and taller! By the time the plan was complete, the Chrysler Building was designed to be 68 stories and 808 feet tall!

However, another architect was designing a skyscraper for New York, and he was determined that *his* building would be the tallest!

Chapter Two

The New York architect who was designing the other building was Harold Craig Severance. Severance was a former business partner of William Van Alen; however, their business relationship did not end well. Now Severance and Van Alen were rivals. And Severance did not want to see his rival design a taller building than his!

Severance's original plan for his building was to make it 60 stories tall. However, he changed his plans, making it 62 stories tall and 840 feet. His building, located at 40 Wall Street, was now 32 feet taller than the Chrysler Building. Then the architect added *another* 65 feet to the building's height!

The two rival architects were both backed by big money. Chrysler Corporation was one of the top auto companies in America and in the 1920s car production boomed. More and more families were able to afford and purchase cars.

The man behind the money for 40 Wall Street was banker George Ohrstrom. The building was designed to be the banking headquarters for the Bank of Manhattan. The building was named the Bank of Manhattan Trust Building.

The two architects, now rivals, both wanted to claim the fame of designing the tallest building in the world and it was a race to the sky!

In April 1930, when the Bank of Manhattan Trust Building was completed, it was 925 feet tall: the tallest building in the world. However, the Bank of Manhattan Trust Building would only remain the world's tallest building for a few months! William Van Alen had a secret plan that he managed to keep out of the news and away from his rival's eyes.

Chapter Three

Van Alen did not want Severance's building to top him, but he knew if his plans for the Chrysler Building became public, his competitor would try to top him again. To make the Chrysler Building taller, he planned to add the now-famous 125-foot spire - but managed to keep it a secret during construction!

You would think that keeping a 125-foot spire a secret would be difficult, but Van Alen was smart! He hid the construction of the spire by building it inside the building in smaller pieces. Once The Manhattan Trust Building was completed, Van Alen had his workers add the smaller pieces and assemble the spire at the top of the building.

When the Chrysler Building opened on May 27, 1930, it was the tallest building in the world, measuring 1,046 feet tall. It would only hold the title for 11 months before yet another building would surpass it. But even though it did not hold the title for long, the Chrysler Building's chrome and bejeweled top shines and glistens in the sun to this day and is recognizable to people all over the world!

Chapter Four

In April 1929, a third building entered the race to claim the title of tallest building in the world. It was the building we now know as the Empire State Building, perhaps the most famous building in New York City. The Empire State Building has been featured in hundreds of movies and is one of the most popular tourist attractions in the city.

Each year, four million people visit the famous building; many of these people ride elevators to the observation decks on the 86th and 102nd floors. On clear days, visitors on the observation decks can see as far as 80 miles away. That means you could see as far as Pennsylvania or Massachusetts!

Construction on the Empire State Building officially began on March 17, 1930. It took an incredibly short one year and 45 days to build. Workers spent over seven million hours constructing the Empire State Building.

When construction on the Empire State Building was completed, it had won the race to the sky and stood a massive 103 stories tall and 1,250 feet to the top floor. The building stands an additional 204 feet tall because of its antenna, for a total height of 1454 feet! It was officially the tallest building in the world!

The Empire State Building remained the tallest building in the world until 1973 when the World Trade Center was constructed. Sadly, the Empire State Building became the tallest building in New York City again on September 11, 2001, when the World Trade Center buildings both collapsed in an attack.

However, by September 2001, many other buildings had been constructed around the world, so even though it was again the tallest building in New York City, the Empire State Building was not the tallest building in the world.

The title of tallest building in New York changed hands again in 2012 when One World Trade Center was completed. One World Trade Center is 104 stories and 1,362 feet without its observation deck or antenna. With the addition of the observation deck and antenna, the massive building stands 1,776 feet tall!

Today the tallest building in the world is the Burji Khalifa in Dubai at 2,717 feet.

Many architects and builders wanted to claim the title of the tallest building in the world, but in the end, only one building could stand on top. The creation of these buildings employed thousands of men at a time when work was scarce.

The Great Depression, a time of struggle for millions of Americans, began in the middle of 1929. The construction race to the sky supplied jobs to thousands of people much in need of work, to support their families.

Although the work was dangerous, men competed for the jobs. Because not only did working on one of these great buildings mean steady work, but it also meant they were working on a piece of history!

Reading Comprehension Questions for:

Race to the Sky - The Chrysler and Empire State Buildings

1. Why is the 1920s referred to as the Roaring Twenties?

2. The story tells us that the two architects Van Alen and Severance were *rivals*. What does the word rival mean?

3. For how long was the Chrysler Building the tallest building in the world? Why did it lose the title?

4. Which building won the race to the sky and became the tallest building in the world?

5. Why do you think the story is called *Race to the Sky*?

The Cousins from Down Under

Chapter One

Flora's mom had been planning their vacation for months. This was going to be a very big trip. Flora and her mom were headed to Australia for two weeks in December. Flora was very excited, but Australia was so far away. It was on the other side of the planet. She knew they'd be flying on three different planes - and the trip would take almost 30 hours!

Flora had never been on a plane ride longer than four hours, so she was nervous about what she would do. Her mom told her not to worry, they would sleep some of the time and the plane offered free movies, games, and TV shows to watch. Plus, Flora could play games, listen to music on her phone, or read one of the three books she was packing. Flora never traveled anywhere without a book, even on vacation. You never knew when you'd have time to spare and could fill it with reading!

Flora's mom had special airplane pillows and blankets packed and lots of their favorite snacks. Plus, her mom told her they would get meals on the plane and during one of their layovers be able to eat at a restaurant in the airport.

There were a lot of things that made Flora excited about this trip. Seeing Australia was going to be amazing. But the thing Flora was most excited about was meeting her cousins for the first time. Flora had two cousins, twins, who were born in Australia - and she had never met them!

Her cousins Ellie and Isla were ten, one year younger than her, and she was going to meet them for the very first time! Her Aunt

Iris was her mom's younger sister and she had moved to Australia 12 years ago.

Aunt Iris was a zoologist and worked at Sydney's Taronga Zoo. Flora had met her aunt twice before when she visited America for work, but she'd only ever talked to her cousins on the computer. She knew what they looked like, she knew what their voices sounded like, and she knew their favorite colors and favorite bands, but she had never met them in person. This was going to be a very exciting trip!

Chapter Two

The more Flora and her mom prepared for the trip, the more excited she became. Flora asked her mom a lot of questions.

"What if we see a giant snake?"

"What if a poisonous spider crawls into my room?"

"Does the water really flush the opposite way in the toilet?"

"Do they have McDonald's there?"

"Will I see a koala? What about a kangaroo?"

"Why is it summer there if it is winter here?"

"What if one of our flights is delayed?"

"What if we run out of sunscreen?"

"Do they drive on the opposite side of the road like England?"

"Will my phone work there?"

And many, many more. Flora's mom tried to answer her questions as best she could, but she mostly just assured Flora that if any problems arose, they would solve them. After all, they were staying with family and would have help.

On the day of the trip, Flora helped her mom load two suitcases and two carry-on bags into the back of the taxi and then they were off!

Their first flight left from Cleveland, the closest city to her home. From Cleveland, they would fly to Houston Texas. In Houston, they had three hours before their next flight. Then from Houston, they would fly to Auckland, New Zealand. The flight would take 14 hours! Then after another hour and a half at the airport in Auckland, they would board their third and final plane for a three-hour flight to Sydney.

It was the 14-hour flight that worried Flora the most. But her mom had done it once before and said if she could sleep some of it, it wouldn't feel that bad. Flora hoped that was true!

As they boarded their first flight, Flora felt the tingle of excitement rise through her belly and into her chest. She and her mom had talked about this trip for so many months. She could hardly believe it was finally here! It was late in the afternoon, and she'd been waiting all day. Flora was full of energy as she walked onto the plane and found her seat.

Chapter Three

In the Houston airport, Flora and her mom found a popular Texas steakhouse chain and ate a delicious and very late dinner. Then they walked around the airport terminal several times to stretch their legs before their long flight. Their long flight to New Zealand was scheduled to leave in 90 minutes, so they had plenty of time to relax, window shop, and get ready!

Boarding the second flight was just as exciting as boarding the first. Only this time, all the flight attendants had cool accents. Flora couldn't tell if they were Australian or New Zealand accents, but they sounded neat to her!

After the onboard safety announcements and take-off, Flora browsed the movie selections. It was too early to sleep, and she wanted to use her time wisely. Flora watched a funny cartoon film and enjoyed the snack the airline passed out. Then she read for a while, and soon it was time for dinner! Her body was telling her it was almost midnight, so eating dinner felt odd. The food smelled good, but there was no room to spread out and she almost knocked her Coke onto her mom's lap. Luckily, she caught it in time!

After dinner, the cabin lights were turned off so people could sleep. Flora felt sleepy and curled up next to the window with the blanket and pillow her mom packed. She listened to soft music inside her headphones and the gentle thrumming of the plane engine lulled her to sleep.

When she woke up, there were lights on and people talking. Flora smelled food and coffee and yawned widely. She felt groggy and a little confused.

"Morning, sleepyhead!" Her mom said.

"What time is it?" Flora asked.

"Well," her mom said, "That's a little confusing because we keep changing time zones, but you slept about six hours, and we will land in about three hours. It's best not to think of actual times right now. That will help you adjust better once we arrive!"

Flora was even more confused, but she said OK and stretched and yawned. After breakfast and another movie, Flora and her mom finally landed in New Zealand. Now there was just one more quick plane change, another three-hour flight, and then finally Australia and meeting her cousins!

Chapter Four

Flora stepped off the plane in Australia and sighed. She had made it! She was groggy, jet-lagged, and sick of airplane food and snacks yet still excited. Flora's mom told her they were meeting Aunt Iris at the baggage claim and then it was a quick drive from the airport to her home in Sydney.

When her mom saw her sister, she ran toward her, and the two women squealed and hugged. In the 12 years since her Aunt Iris had moved to Australia, her mom had only seen her four times. Once when the twins were born, her mom went to Australia for two weeks to help, twice when Aunt Iris visited the U.S. for work, and once when they both went to their cousin's wedding in Florida. Flora knew that this trip was extra special because the sisters were getting time together.

Flora didn't have a sister. It was just her, her mom and her dad. That's part of the reason she was so excited to meet her cousins!

Aunt Iris gave Flora a huge hug and said, "You have grown so much since I last saw you!"

Flora beamed and blushed at the same time.

Then her aunt said, "Let's get you two to the house so you can see the girls and freshen up!"

It was already 7 p.m. in Australia, so luckily Flora wouldn't have to wait too long for bedtime because she was exhausted!

Chapter Five

When they stepped outside, Flora was shocked by how warm it was. But then she remembered it was summer here even though it was December. When they got to Aunt Iris's car, the driver's seat was on the opposite side. It looked so odd! Flora realized they did drive on the opposite side of the road, and the entire drive she felt like she was in a topsy-turvy world.

Aunt Iris lived in a tall apartment building in downtown Sydney. Flora had never lived in an apartment or a city; she wondered what it was like. Her Uncle Bernie, whom Flora had only met once, greeted them in the lobby and helped with the suitcases. He gave Flora a high-five. They rode up 15 flights in a lift and then walked down a long, carpeted hallway.

"We're here!" Aunt Iris said and she opened a blue door with 1526 in silver numbering on the front. Standing right inside were Flora's cousins!

"You're here!" The twins squealed together and rushed to hug Flora. All three girls started jumping up and down. "Come with us!" Isla said, pulling Flora's arm. "Our room is this way!" The girls scampered down the hallway, giggling as they went.

Isla and Ellie's room was seafoam green and covered in posters. Some of the people, Flora recognized, but there were bands and sports stars she had never heard of before. The three cousins sat on the soft, cream carpet that covered the floor and quickly started chatting about their plans for the next two weeks.

Isla and Ellie had two more days of school until their holiday break began, but they told Flora that they would go to the beach on Christmas Eve for a barbeque. Flora laughed. The idea of visiting the beach for Christmas sounded so strange. She told her cousins how they usually went caroling all bundled up and drank hot chocolate by the fireplace.

"That sounds so weird!" Isla said. "I can't imagine a cold Christmas!"

They discussed other things they wanted to do like take Flora to the zoo with their mom for a behind-the-scenes tour, go to the art museum, visit Luna Park and ride the giant Ferris wheel, and see the Christmas show at the Sydney Opera House.

Flora started to yawn, and her eyes glazed over. Her brain was overwhelmed but in a good way. She told her cousins she was looking forward to everything but right now what she was most looking forward to was a shower and a long, restful sleep!

The girls laughed and showed her the room she'd be sleeping in with her mom. Uncle Bernie had already placed their suitcases on the two twin beds. Flora closed the door and sighed a deep sigh. Meeting her cousins was as good as she had imagined, and she knew the rest of the trip would be wonderful too!

Reading Comprehension Questions for:
My Cousins from Down Under

1. Where are Flora and her mom going on vacation? Why are they going there?

2. Why is Flora so excited about her vacation?

3. Why was Flora's mom so happy to see her sister, Flora's Aunt Iris?

4. How did Flora's cousins react when they saw her?

5. What do you think Flora did after the story ended? Why do you think that?

The Transatlantic Crossing

Chapter One

Mary stood on the edge of the wharf and craned her neck up to look at the gigantic ocean liner, the *RMS Majestic*. It was the world's largest ocean liner. The ship had three golden funnels looming upward from the middle and its large black hull looked like a giant wall.

Mary took a deep breath, smoothed the pleats of her skirt and jacket, and picked up her cardboard suitcase. For three years Mary had skimped and saved every coin possible to purchase her ticket for this journey. The ticket cost $124 and left her with only $40 in her pocket once she reached America.

Her cousin Kate had moved to New York two years ago and Mary would be sharing a small, studio apartment with her and Kate's friend Jane once she arrived. It would cost her $20 a month, half the money she possessed. But Mary wasn't nervous. She was smart and had graduated from high school. She'd moved to England at the age of 18 to work in a factory during the war. Mary had brains and skills and was confident she'd find employment once in America.

But first, she had to get there. She took another deep breath, patted her jacket pocket to ensure her ticket and documents were inside, and joined the long line of third-class passengers waiting to board the gigantic ship.

Chapter Two

Mary slowly moved up the gangplank waiting for her turn. She wasn't shy by nature, but she heard so many different accents and languages around her she felt out of place. She didn't know who she'd be sharing a cabin with, all she knew was that it would be other women.

She wondered what it would be like to share a cabin with women who didn't speak English. Would she feel lonely or enjoy the time to herself? She didn't have much packed in her suitcase, but she did bring two of her favorite books. Having her books with her in her new home would be comforting among so many unfamiliar things. The two books she packed were *The Wonderful Wizard of Oz* and *Emma*. If nothing else, she could read on the boat.

The transatlantic journey would take less than a week. The boat left from South Hampton, England, and would arrive at New York Harbor in only five or six days depending on the weather.

The *RMS Majestic* belonged to the White Star Line, the same shipping company that had built and launched the infamous *Titanic* ten years earlier. But that didn't worry Mary.

She, of course, remembers the news of the *Titanic's* fatal maiden voyage. In fact, it was built in Belfast, where Mary grew up. Many of her older cousins, and the fathers of some of her friends, had worked on building the great ship.

But there hadn't been a tragedy like that in a decade. The *Titanic's* sinking had meant changes that made ocean liners safer in many ways. Now there were more lifeboats and lifeboat practice drills, ice patrols in the North Atlantic, and onboard radios were now staffed at all times.

All these thoughts and more passed through Mary's mind as she moved up the gangplank waiting her turn to board.

Finally, she was at the top. She handed over her ticket and papers for inspection and waited anxiously. There was no reason to be anxious, but Mary simply wanted to get on board, find her cabin, and settle in.

"Welcome aboard the *Majestic* and have a safe journey," the officer told her.

Mary politely said, "Thank you," and walked on board.

Chapter Three

Once on board, Mary examined her ticket looking for her cabin number. She had it memorized, of course - it had been memorized for a week since she purchased her ticket! It was F-Deck, section 119, Berth #1. But she wanted to read it again to reassure herself. The ship was massive, and she did not want to become lost. Mary paused and read the signs on the wall and took the first left. She followed signs, walking down narrow passageways, turning right and left until at last she found her tiny cabin.

The door was open and someone was already inside. A young woman, about Mary's age, was laying a suitcase on one of the lower beds. Mary gently knocked on the open door.

The woman turned and smiled. "Oh hello!" She said with a lilting Irish accent. "My name is Bess, well Elisabeth, but everyone calls me Bess!"

Mary felt comforted by hearing an Irish accent, although it did not sound like this woman came from Belfast like her.

"Hello, I'm Mary," she replied.

The other woman beamed. "Oh, you're Irish like me! How wonderful. I'm from Dublin myself, but moved to London after the war. You?"

"I moved to Southampton, during the war, to work in a munitions factory. Then I stayed in the city afterwards but moved to secretarial work. I've been saving for my ticket for three years," Mary explained.

"I bet you have!" Bess said. "I worked as a secretary myself for the *Evening News*, but I want to be a reporter. That's why I am moving to New York, to be like Nellie Blye or Loulou Lassen!"

Mary had heard of Nellie Blye, but she wondered who Loulou Lassen was and asked.

"Oh!" Bess said. "She's a Dutch journalist. Well, she was, I don't know if she writes anymore, but still, a female journalist!"

Mary laughed; she couldn't help it. Bess's energy was contagious. She placed her suitcase on the bed above Bess's, which was indicated as Berth #1.

"Let's go roam the ship!" Bess said, linking her arm through Mary's.

Mary made sure her money was secure in her jacket pocket and glanced at her suitcase to make sure it was tied shut. Then she nodded an OK and off they went!

Chapter Four

The young women wound their way through the maze of hallways that made up the third class. There were no windows at this level, so it was a bit dark and lit by electric light only. People were shouting, laughing, and talking in all different languages and the sound was hurting Mary's ears. The boat hadn't even left yet and already she was feeling closed-in. She hoped that the mood and volume would quiet down once everyone settled and became used to their lodgings.

The *Majestic* was advertised as an Ocean Palace, but Mary knew the luxury was reserved for those in first class. Nonetheless, the third-class areas were quite nice. She read that there was even a swimming pool on board for those in first class! The idea seemed funny to her. Swimming in a pool in the middle of the ocean.

The girls wandered until they found the third-class lounge. It was a cheerful but simple room with a few small couches, desks with chairs, and windows with actual sunlight coming in. Mary knew she'd probably spend time here reading and enjoying the light.

Mary and Bess sat on a couch near a window so they could watch as the massive ocean liner sailed away from England's coast. Mary didn't know if she'd ever see England or Ireland again and wanted to take one last glimpse.

The two women talked and got to know one another as they sipped tea that was offered in the lounge. Mary learned that Bess had two sisters and two brothers and that she was the oldest and was 22, three years younger than Mary.

Bess told her she loved reading and writing from a young age, even though her father discouraged it and wanted her to find work at 14 to help support the family. Her father allowed her to stay in school until she was 16, and then she worked at a pub washing tables and serving food. In her free time, she would write poetry and short stories about the men who came into the pub.

After the war, when she was 18, Bess moved to London so she could make more money and send extra home to help her family. Now she was ready to do the same in an even bigger city!

Mary was inspired by Bess's energy and enthusiasm. Mary had two sisters herself. One was older and married and the other was younger and still at home. Mary began work at the age of 14, working in a laundry in the city.

Now, at 25, Mary was considered an old maid, but that didn't bother her; she dreamed of bigger things than marriage and housework. Not that she looked down on any woman who did those things - it just wasn't the life for her.

As the women continued their walk and strolled the third-class decks breathing in the salty sea air, Mary was glad to have already made a friend. It would make the journey and arriving in a new city more enjoyable.

Chapter Five

Mary and Bess shared their cabin with two other young women, Jill from England and Chloe from France. Chloe also spoke English well and was able to join in the fun conversations. All four of the young women dreamed of exciting lives in New York and had big plans. As Mary got to know each of these women better, she hoped each of their dreams would come true.

They spent hours walking around the third-class decks, playing games of cards in the lounge, and talking late into the night on their bunks. The sailing was smooth, the weather was calm and clear. Because it was summer, it was often warm and pleasant on the decks during the day but would turn chilly at night. When Mary couldn't sleep, she would climb out of her bunk quietly to not wake her roommates and visit the decks. There she would lean on the railing, breathing in the cool, salty, night air and dreaming of America.

On the day the ship arrived at New York Harbor, it was warm and sunny. Mary stood at the deck railing and stared in awe at the size of the city. How would she ever find her way around this massive place? She felt a tingle of nerves but reminded herself she had worked through and survived a war, so surely, she could navigate some city streets.

As the liner sailed closer to the harbor, she saw hundreds of people waiting. Her cousin Kate was supposed to be among them. Mary took a deep breath. She had no idea what adventures and challenges faced her in this new and foreign city, but she knew that she was ready.

Reading Comprehension Questions for:
The Transatlantic Crossing

1. The story tells us Mary only had $40 in cash when she reached America. Mary's story is set in 1922, so $40 would be about the same as $750 today. Do you think $750 would be enough money to move to a different country? Why or why not?

2. The story is called *The Transatlantic Crossing*. What does *transatlantic* mean?

3. What are the three ways that the sinking of the *Titanic* led to changes, that made ocean liners safer?

4. When did Mary move to Southampton? What did she do there?

5. What are some things Bess and Mary have in common? What are some things that are different?

6. A few times in the story, Mary takes a deep breath. Once is before boarding the ship, and another is before leaving the ship. Why do you think she does this?

Mrs. Butters and
the Haunted House

Chapter One

All the kids who lived in Maplesville knew to avoid the old McKinnley mansion. The massive house sat high on a high hill at the far edge of town. There were a lot of rumors about the house, and no one knew what to believe. Some people said it was the scene of a horrible crime years and years ago. Others said it was haunted by ghosts. A third popular rumor was that a family of vampires lived in the house, and that's why you never saw anyone come in or out during the day.

The truth was, no one really knew what went on at the McKinley mansion, you just didn't go there. Occasionally lights could be seen, glowing softly from the windows. Was that the ghosts or the vampires? The lawn was overrun with weeds and there was an old iron gate at the front of the driveway. The iron gate was the furthest anyone ever went.

Older kids and teens would dare one another to see who could get the closest to the house. These bets were usually made around Halloween when everything felt extra spooky. But no one was ever brave enough to go past the gate. The unlucky person, pretending to be brave, would slowly walk up to the gate, touch it, and then run away.

That is exactly what was happening one cool, October night when an old black car came down the driveway, the gravel crunching under the wheels. Zach, Perry, and Ghia were waiting by a large maple tree, one of the many the town was supposedly named for, as their friend Miguel crept up the driveway.

All of a sudden, Miguel came running back to them yelling, "Hide!"

The four kids quickly ducked behind the tree trunk as the car passed.

"Who was that?!" Ghia exclaimed. "I've never seen anyone come or go from this house before."

"I have no idea," Miguel said. "I heard the car and ran. Did anyone see who was driving it?"

"It was too dark, man," Zach replied, shrugging his shoulders. "I couldn't see anything."

"Maybe it was a ghost!" Perry said.

"A ghost driving a car?" Asked Ghia.

"Yeah," agreed Zach, "doesn't seem likely."

"Then why were you all so scared?" Perry pointed out.

"I just didn't want to get caught!" Miguel responded.

"Yeah, sure," Perry scoffed. "You all believe in the stories as much as I do."

"I mean, it *is* weird," Ghia said. "No one ever comes or goes from here; something is definitely up."

"Let's come back tomorrow and see if it happens again!" Zach suggested.

The four friends all agreed to meet back at the corner of the street at 8 p.m. the next night to see if the mysterious car appeared again.

Chapter Two

The next night, the four teens met on the corner of Maplewood and Vine and then walked to the giant tree at the base of the McKinley mansion driveway.

"Does anyone know why this is called the McKinley mansion?" Perry asked.

"I always assumed some rich family named McKinley owned it at some point," Ghia replied.

The boys all nodded at her response; it made sense to them.

"But no one lives here, right?" Zach asked.

The rest all shrugged. There had never been a *For Sale* or *For Rent* sign posted. The car last night was the first time any of them had seen anyone driving to or from the house, and Ghia lived right down the road.

"But, I mean, there's lights on sometimes, right, Ghia? So, someone must live here," Zach continued.

Miguel snuck up behind him and grabbed him saying, "Unless it's the ghosts!"

Zach jumped and playfully hit his friend's arm. "Don't do that, man!"

"What, are you afraid of ghosts?" Miguel teased.

"No, I just don't like people sneaking up on me!" Zach said.

"Will you two knock it off?" Perry hissed. "We need to be quiet so we can hear if the car comes."

The four kids sat on the ground behind the giant maple but a line of sight to the driveway.

After 20 minutes, Zach said, "This is boring, no one is coming." He started to stand up.

Just then Perry said, "Shhhh!", and motioned for his friend to sit down.

Then they all heard the sound of the gravel under car tires. The same black car was slowly driving down the driveway toward them. They scrambled to climb behind the tree before the headlights caught them in their glare.

"OK, that's two nights in a row," Ghia said. "Something is definitely going on up at the mansion. And the only way we're going to find out is if we get closer tomorrow. Meet back at the corner at 7:30, just after dark. We're going to get a closer look."

The friends all nodded nervously. Although, it was just a house and a car. What was there to be nervous about?

Chapter Three

At 7:30, all four friends met again at the corner. They weren't exactly sure what they were looking for, but they knew something strange was happening at the old mansion and wanted to be the ones to figure it out. It was kind of like being a detective!

"OK, here's the plan," Ghia began, "we're going to go all the way up to the house and look and listen for anything that might be a clue."

"Like what?" Perry asked.

"Like garbage cans indicating someone lives there, or the sound of a TV or music inside," Ghia explained.

"Eww, I am *not* looking in someone's garbage cans," Zach said.

Ghia rolled her eyes. Zach was always so dramatic. "Do you want to figure this out or not?" Ghia persisted. "There has to be a reason a car has been at the house two nights in a row!"

"Fine. Whatever," Zach mumbled.

The four teens slowly and quietly walked up the driveway, listening for the sound of the car in case they quickly needed to hide. When they reached the top, they saw the car parked on the side of the house and one window light at the back.

"Is anyone in the car?" Perry whispered.

Miguel peeked into the window and shook his head no.

Just then, they heard a terrible wailing, like a ghost. They dashed behind a tall bush and hid.

They all looked at each other, questioning what they had just heard, but no one had an answer. Then they heard the sound again. It definitely sounded like someone or something crying - but who or what?

The sound stopped and a few minutes later they heard the front door open and close. A tall man dressed all in black and carrying a large black bag climbed into the black car and drove away.

Then the house was silent. The light that had been on before was now off. Just as the teens were about to climb out of their hiding spot, they heard a voice singing. It was a soft, high voice, but they couldn't understand the words.

"That's it, I'm out of here!" Zach said and he got up and left.

His friends followed him. When they reached the road, they all looked at each other.

"It's definitely ghosts," Zach stated. "That wailing and then the weird singing with no lights on?"

"Yeah. I don't know. It's very strange," Miguel added. "I'm not going back."

"Me neither," piped up Perry.

Ghia, however, wasn't convinced. She didn't believe in ghosts or that the house was haunted. There had to be a logical explanation and she wanted to find out what it was. Without telling her friends, she made plans to go back to the house alone.

Chapter Four

They're being ridiculous, Ghia thought to herself as she climbed up the driveway the next day. She'd decided to go to the house in daylight and simply knock on the front door. If there was anyone living there, she figured, they would simply answer.

When she reached the front door, Ghia raised her hand to knock but then paused. *I'm all alone up here and no one knows I'm here*, she thought. *What if something bad happens?* But Ghia quickly shook the thoughts out of her head, raised her hand again, and knocked.

The door echoed loudly and then she waited. At first, she didn't hear anything, yet just as she was about to turn away, she heard a strange scuffling noise behind the door. It was a click-clack sound, like nails tapping on a chalkboard. Then she heard a quiet voice say, "Just a moment."

The door swung inward and a short, elderly woman holding onto a harness attached to a large, golden retriever stood there. "Yes?" The woman said.

Ghia stared; this was not what she expected.

"Who's there?" The woman said. "I can hear you breathing."

"Oh," Ghia gasped. "I'm Ghia, I live a few doors down. I...um...I." Ghia stumbled for words. "I saw a car leave your house the last few nights and I had never seen a car here before, so I was just checking that, um..."

"Ahhh. So, you were curious if the house is haunted, like the rumors say," the woman replied. "I can assure you: The house isn't haunted. Me and Binx live here. I've lived here for the past 75 years."

"You have?" Ghia asked. "But there are never any lights on and that was the first time I've seen a car!"

"Well," said the woman. "I am blind, so I do not need lights. And I do have groceries and other things delivered here and there. But I don't drive. I have a huge property, so I take Binx for walks and have very little need to visit the town. But I do get lonely."

Ghia didn't know what to say. So, she told the truth. "You're right, kids do think your house is haunted. I'm embarrassed to admit it, but my friends and I snuck up here last night and thought we heard crying and singing. It definitely sounded mysterious!"

"Well now," the woman said. "I'm a little embarrassed someone heard all that, but I do appreciate your honesty. Would you like to come in for a cup of tea? I can tell you all about my crying and singing, and I would really enjoy the company."

Ghia accepted and followed the woman through the old house.

It turned out the woman's name was Mrs. Butters. She had inherited the house from its former owner, Mason McKinley, whose great-grandfather had built the house nearly 200 years ago.

"I grew up in this house, you see," Mrs. Butters told Ghia over a couple of cups of Earl Gray tea. "My mother was the housekeeper for Mr. Mason McKinley, and then when she retired, I took over the job, about, oh, 50 years ago. I was quite young. But a few years later, I began to lose my sight. Mr. Mickinley paid for me to see all the best doctors, but no one could fix it. So eventually I went blind."

"That's terrible!" Ghia exclaimed.

"It was indeed unfortunate. But Mr. Mason had known me my whole life and treated me like family. He never married or had children of his own. So, in a way, my sister and I were like children to him. My sister moved away and married, and he invited me to stay here. Anyway, when he passed away 30 years ago, he left the house to me, and I've lived here alone ever since. Sometimes my nieces and nephews visit or call, but mostly it's just me and my dog.

"That's why I was crying the other night. The vet had come to visit and Binx here is very ill. That was the vet in the car you saw drive away. Binx likes it when I sing to him, so I do that to make him feel better."

Ghia reached out and placed her hand on top of Mrs. Butters's. "I had no idea anyone lived here. I am sorry you've been so lonely. May I visit again?"

Mrs. Butters's eyes teared up. "I would love that, dear!"

So, from then on, twice a week, Ghia would visit Mrs. Butters after school. She would run errands for her and help in any way possible. When her friends started asking about where she was going all the time, she would just smile and say she was busy.

Eventually, Ghia would tell the boys about Mrs. Butters and the house, but for now, she enjoyed being the only one who wasn't scared of the big mansion on the hill.

Reading Comprehension Questions for:
Mrs. Butters and the Haunted House

1. Was the house haunted? What was really going on?

2. Do you think the teens really believed there were ghosts? Why or why not?

3. Why do you think Mrs. Butters spent so much time alone instead of coming to town?

4. What do you think happens after the story finishes?

The Magical
Properties of Plants

Chapter One

Did you know that plants are magical? Well, they are! They aren't magical in the way we think of magic spells or fairytales, but plants can and do many wonderful things.

First, and you probably already know this, plants are food. They are not only food for us, but they are food for millions of animals too!

Second, plants can heal us. Many plants have medicinal properties and are used as medicines. Humans have been using plants for thousands of years to cure illnesses, reduce fever, calm rashes, and much more!

Third, plants provide us with oxygen and keep our planet healthy and thriving. Without plants, there would be no people or animals. That is why it is so important to treat forests, jungles, and wildlife areas well.

Plants are also good for our mental health and relieve stress. Being around plants can actually make you feel better.

Lastly, some of your favorite plants can also keep unwanted critters like mosquitoes and wasps away! So, if you have a big problem at home, you can plant and grow specific plants to ward off those pesky bugs.

There are so many amazing things plants can do for us that they truly are magical!

Chapter Two

The most common thing plants can do for us is feed us. We eat plants every day! Fresh strawberries and grapes in our fruit salad, delicious pumpkin pie at Thanksgiving and Christmas, refreshing fruit smoothies, and crisp green salads are just a few of the ways plants feed us.

But did you know that each and every different type of plant we eat does something magical for our body? If you've ever heard the expression "Eat the rainbow," it means to eat a variety of fresh fruits and veggies.

Each color of the rainbow provides benefits to our bodies. Red and pink plants like strawberries and raspberries are high in vitamin C and good for our hearts and brains. Orange foods like carrots and oranges are also high in vitamin C, making them heart-healthy foods. But they're also full of beta-carotene, which helps our eyes. Have you ever seen a rabbit with glasses?

Green foods, the ones kids and many adults avoid the most, are some of the most magical plants we should eat. They have vitamins A, B, C, E, and K!

They improve your heart and brain health, help you heal faster from illness and injury, and support your bone health.

So, while you may not want to eat that broccoli or those Brussel sprouts, you should give them a try!

Blue and purple foods like blueberries, eggplant, and purple cabbage are best for boosting your brain power because of their powerful antioxidants. These magical foods boost memory, focus, and attention span.

Even white and brown foods not traditionally considered part of the food rainbow have benefits! Garlic, mushrooms, onions, and ginger are full of disease-fighting nutrients to keep you healthy and strong.

So, the next time your parents serve you fruits and veggies, remember all the magical properties they contain and how they boost your brain and body!

Chapter Three

One of the most magical things plants can do is heal us. The human race has used plants as medicine for tens of thousands of years, and many cultures today still rely on natural remedies over the ones at the drugstore. However, you should always follow your doctor's advice when treating an illness!

But if you have some minor scrapes and bumps at home, there are several ways plants can help. Aloe, for example, is perfect for treating sunburn or irritated skin.

The soothing cool gel magically relieves the painful sensation of a bad sunburn!

Essential oils like peppermint, rosemary, and lavender relieve headaches and reduce stress. You can also grow fresh peppermint, lavender, and rosemary inside your home to keep it smelling fresh and soothing.

Lemon, ginger, and honey are ideal when suffering from a cough, cold, or sore throat. All three are common ingredients in cough drops, cold medicine, and teas. So, the next time you have a bad cough that won't go away, try a spoonful of honey!

Have you ever heard of the plant wooly lamb's ear? This plant isn't meant to be eaten or made into tea; instead, it can be used as a bandage for scrapes and cuts. It is nature's original band-aid. Pretty magical indeed!

Instead of a lamb's ear, how about a pig's ear to treat warts? This funny-looking plant can be used to treat warts on your feet or hands, but a trip to the doctor is probably easier and quicker...

And speaking of warts, St. John's Wort is a plant with anti-bacterial properties that can treat skin infections. It is also beneficial in treating depression and anxiety.

Licorice is an excellent remedy for tummy troubles. And no, we don't mean that red, stringy candy you buy at the grocery store. The licorice plant tastes like black jellybeans!

These are just a few of the examples of the amazing medicinal properties plants have.

However, you should never take a natural remedy or eat an unknown plant without a parent or doctor's permission. Some plants are dangerous to humans and can make you ill or even cause death!

Chapter Four

You've probably learned in school that plants and trees provide us with oxygen - and that is pretty magical! The fact that our planet had the precise conditions necessary to create plant life is astounding to begin with. Now there are millions of different types of plants on Earth.

And being surrounded by plants doesn't only make the air we breathe cleaner; it also reduces stress. Doctors and scientists have proven that being around plants and nature is good for our physical and mental health.

Consider keeping plants in your home, or helping your parents maintain a garden. The act of caring for plants is brain-boosting, too. Plus, the vitamin D your body will receive from being out in the sun will help boost your mood as well!

Another benefit to keeping plants in your home is that they can keep away pesky bugs like mice, spiders, and mosquitoes. Most critters hate the smell of peppermint. So, if you want a critter-free zone in your house, use peppermint spray around the windows or doors. Or better yet, keep fresh peppermint plants inside!

Other plants like lavender will keep rabbits and deer out of your garden. And mosquitoes hate rosemary!

Plants have so many magical properties and do so much to benefit our lives. Show your appreciation for plants by enjoying a fresh smoothie, going for a walk, drinking a cup of peppermint tea, and treating the plants you see with respect and kindness!

Reading Comprehension Questions for:
The Magical Properties of Plants

1. What are some of the things the story mentions plants can do that are "magical"?

2. Pick one of the colors of the rainbow. What are some foods from that color and what benefits do they provide?

3. What are some ways plants can help us when we're sick or injured?

4. What is something new that you learned about plants from reading this story?

Conclusion

We hope you enjoyed these fun and uniquely crafted stories for fifth-grade readers. Each story was broken into mini-chapters to assist with reading comprehension. These chapters were designed to be slightly shorter than a standard book chapter to help you focus on reading comprehension, memory, and retention. Some books you may already be reading likely have lengthier chapters several pages long!

Every story in this book uses common sight words fifth-grade level readers will recognize or can decipher using context clues. But there are also some new and challenging or unfamiliar words to help push you to the next level! Remember, it is OK if you do not know how to say a word or what it means. Reading and hearing new words is how you learn them.

But stories do much more than teach words. Stories engage your imagination and teach you to dream of new and exciting things. Stories teach you about new people and places and help you learn about yourselves too. Some stories evoke adventure, some teach valuable lessons about family and friendship, while others are simply fun to read!

When you read a story, it opens windows to new ways of thinking. What did you learn while reading these stories? Did you discover anything new about yourself or someone you may know? Do you have a favorite story in the book? Which one and why?

We encourage you to read your favorites again and again! Just like watching your favorite movie over and over, it is an awesome idea to re-read your favorite stories. The more you read a story, the more familiar the words become, the faster your flow becomes, and the more you comprehend or understand.

In addition to language and literacy skills, reading promotes problem-solving and other cognitive skills. We encourage you to use the guided reading questions at the beginning of this book, which can be applied to any story in the book, to enhance your reading and comprehension skills.

While these stories are designed for fifth-grade readers (ages nine through eleven), older and younger children will enjoy them too!

Happy reading!

Made in the USA
Las Vegas, NV
11 October 2024

96669143R00075